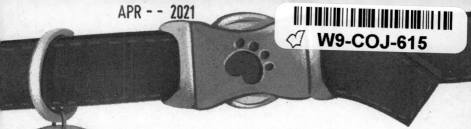

A DOG'S DAY

I AM BELLA,

STAR OF THE SHOW

Catherine Stier

illustrated by
Francesca Rosa

Albert Whitman & Company
Chicago, Illinois

With love to my kind aunt and godmother, Patricia LaPrise.
Your creativity has always inspired me!—CS

To Lorenzo, Stefano, and Silvia. My favorite actors.—FR

Library of Congress Cataloging-in-Publication data
is on file with the publisher.
Text copyright © 2020 by Catherine Stier
Illustrations copyright © 2020 by Albert Whitman & Company
Illustrations by Francesca Rosa
Hardcover edition first published in the United States of America
in 2020 by Albert Whitman & Company
Paperback edition first published in the United States of America in
2021 by Albert Whitman & Company
ISBN 978-0-8075-1680-5 (paperback)
ISBN 978-0-8075-1674-4 (ebook)

Printed in the United States of America
10 9 8 7 6 5 4 3 2 1 LB 24 23 22 21 20

Design by Rick DeMonico

For more information about Albert Whitman & Company,
visit our website at www.albertwhitman.com.

Contents

Chapter 1

Two Dogs, One House

Something is up today. From the tip of my nose to the end of my tail, I can feel excitement in the house this morning. Chewy doesn't seem to notice. He's still curled up in his big doggy bed in the kitchen, snoring away. Typical.

Chewy and I were both adopted years ago from the animal shelter by the Jameson family. I was a full-grown dog that no one else seemed to want when Mom, Dad, and their son, Aidan,

brought me home. By breed, I am a Jack Russell terrier—mostly.

I was adopted first, and I can tell you, I didn't mind being the only dog in the house. A while later, the Jamesons brought home a German shepherd puppy. Even then, Chewy loved to sleep in, eat, and chew on things. That last part is how he got his name. When he was a pup, there were lots of ruined shoes around the house.

And my name? Well, not to brag, but I've been told Bella means "beautiful" in some languages. I happen to think it's a name that suits me just fine.

When Chewy came to live with us, he was already bigger than me, and he just kept growing. I'm little, the smallest of my litter, but I'm very mature. Chewy still acts like a sloppy, silly puppy, even though he's full-grown. We are just about

as different as two dogs can be, but we have one
thing in common: Mom calls us her "star dogs."
That's because we work in what's called show
business—or showbiz, for short.

Both Mom and Aidan are up early this
morning. I'm guessing all the hustle and bustle
means one of us dogs will be heading out to
film with Mom today.

"How about some breakfast, Bella? Then you
and I can work on training a bit before I leave

for school," Aidan says as he comes into the kitchen.

An early breakfast? Without Chewy? That's fine with me. Maybe I'll get to enjoy my food in peace. And I know that word *training* means lots of attention, treats, and praise. I'm on board with that too. I pick up the soft scrap of fabric Mom calls my blankie and prance in circles to show Aidan my happiness with his plans.

As soon as Chewy hears the sound of food being poured into my bowl, though, he's up and alert, and comes to check things out.

"Okay, Chewy, you can have your breakfast too." Aidan laughs as he fills Chewy's bowl.

Chewy does not prance prettily like me. He dives in and devours his food, sending nuggets bouncing from the bowl. Typical.

I, on the other paw, drop my blankie and nibble neatly at my meal.

Chewy and I get along all right, usually. But honestly, I don't see why he gets to go on more filming jobs with Mom than *me*. I mean, he's smart, I guess, but he's also loud and messy sometimes and so immature.

"Don't take it personally, Bella," Mom told me once as she left with Chewy. "It's just that Chewy can play a police dog or guard dog. And lately, there have been lots of shows and movies filming here in Atlanta that call for big dogs."

"Your chance will come," she added. "You're pint-sized, but packed with personality!"

Okay, I admit Chewy can look tough and heroic. But I still don't get why I'm not cast more often. After all, Mom is right about my oversize personality. And I'm a triple threat: I'm cute, clever, and never miss a cue—or a command!

Once I'm done with breakfast, I glance at Chewy. Of all the nerve! He has *my* fuzzy mouse toy clamped in his teeth! I march over and tug it out of his mouth.

Play with your own toys, big guy! I think as I sashay away.

Chewy doesn't grumble. He just goes and finds one of his own big chew bones. As he should!

Then Aidan calls me over to a corner of the kitchen.

"Hey, Bella!" he says. "If we're going to get our new trick right, and if I'm going to be a professional dog trainer like Mom someday, we both need plenty of practice."

Aidan has everything set up on the kitchen floor, ready to go. There's a little toy saucer, a plastic teacup, and a cleanup rag. There's a pitcher of cool water to refill the teacup. Also, Aidan has a handful of treats—I can smell them!

I drop my mouse toy and prance in circles with excitement. I know what all this means. It's time for me to show off my talents!

Chapter 2

Practice Makes Perfect

I scurry over next to Aidan, who is standing near the toy teacup.

First, Aidan says the word *sit*. That's easy. I learned that ages ago. I let my rump fall to the floor, and Aidan makes a little noise with the clicker he holds in his hand. Whenever I hear the sound of the click, I know I've done the action right, and a reward is coming.

What's my favorite reward? Liver treats, definitely. Oh, and I love the cheerful sound of Aidan's voice when he says, "Good doggy!"

Aidan tosses me my treat, and I gobble it up.

"Okay, Bella, now it's time for our special trick," says Aidan. "The one we've been working on all month. The one that will make you a star."

I know what's about to happen, but I wait for the command.

"Tip it," says Aidan. I raise my paw just right, so it nudges the teacup. The cup overturns and water splashes on the tile floor. When I hear the click, I know I've aced it.

"That's it, Bella! That's perfect!" Aidan speaks in his excited voice that makes me happy and wiggly all over, and he gives me my tiny treat. Then he mops up the water with the rag.

I'm glad Aidan is so excited! It took me a

while to perfect this particular action. I needed to learn what was expected first. I mean, humans are usually upset when things get knocked over, right? But for some reason, this is exactly what makes Aidan the happiest.

While Mom taught me other commands and movements, Aidan patiently worked with me

on the tip-it trick before and after school each day. We started first with an action I already knew—how to lift one paw. As I put my paw toward Aidan's hand, I sometimes hit the plastic teacup. Then I'd hear the click and get a treat.

It didn't take me long to figure out that knocking over this particular teacup was a good thing! Soon Aidan added the words *tip it* to our game. Now, whenever Aidan says those words, I know just what to do. I admit, it's fun—but I still don't know how making a mess will make me a star! Since it's Chewy that gets all the roles, maybe I should practice looking fierce and growling on command instead.

Aidan and I try our trick a few more times. Before long, Dad is up too. He grabs a cup of coffee and stops to watch us. It's even better doing my trick with an audience! Then I get even more attention and "good doggy" praise!

"Great job, son," Dad says. I look up at Dad, and he laughs. "My apologies, Bella. Didn't mean to leave you out. You are doing a fine job as well."

"I just hope Bella gets it right when it counts," says Aidan. "Mom is helping me with my dog-training skills. This is the first time she's trusted me to teach Bella a new trick for a filming job. I don't want to let her down."

Don't worry, Aidan! I think. *I promise you can count on me when it matters most—whenever that is!*

"I'm pretty sure you both will make her proud," Dad says.

Aidan nods, refills the teacup, and is ready to start again when the doorbell rings.

At first I figure it's one of Aidan's fifth-grade friends, arriving early to walk with him to the school bus stop.

I do what I always do when I hear the doorbell. I jump up and trot toward the door. Chewy, the copycat, follows close behind.

But I stop short and let out a bark when—*my goodness*—I see strangers on the porch!

Mom throws opens the door.

"Good morning! You are right on time," she says in a cheerful voice to two smiling people.

I wag my tail and greet our guests with a good-morning bark.

No wonder Aidan and Mom were so excited all morning! They knew that new friends were coming over!

Then I see that one of the new friends is holding a big, boxy thing on his shoulder.

I'm enough of a showbiz dog to recognize a camera when I see it!

Chapter 3

Out of the Spotlight

My human family and the people on the porch shake hands.

"I'm Megan Wong, the reporter who contacted you," the first human says.

"And I'm Ed Mendoza. I'll be working the camera. Thank you for inviting our news crew to your home."

News crew? I lean out and sniff these visiting

humans. Chewy, though, hangs back. He is still a bit wary when it comes to new people. He doesn't relax until he sees that Mom is happy to see these visitors.

"You are both most welcome," Mom says as she shows the news crew in.

"Hello, Chewy and Bella." The reporter crouches down, and Chewy and I offer our paws to shake.

"I've heard all about you two. It's an honor to meet such talented dogs," she says.

Dad excuses himself to leave for work, and Mom and Aidan lead the news crew to the kitchen.

"I understand you're a professional dog trainer," the reporter says while the cameraperson fusses with some equipment.

Mom nods. "Yes, I work at a dog-training school and also with these sweeties in my own home."

"They *are* sweet," the reporter agrees. She looks adoringly at Chewy and me.

Thanks for noticing, I think.

As a light on the camera flashes on, the reporter asks Mom, "How did your dogs get their start in acting?"

"My son and I decided it would be fun to work as extras in some of the shows and movies filming here in Atlanta," Mom explains. "We've played customers in an ice-cream parlor and fans cheering at a football game. We had such a good time that I thought our dogs would like to be in movies and shows too. They love nothing better than showing off before an audience!"

"Yes, I can see that they like attention," says the reporter.

"So I contacted an agency for animals that perform on film," Mom says. "Turns out, both dogs have important qualities casting agents look for—they get along with other dogs and people, love to learn new things, and don't get nervous around cameras and other equipment. Best of all, performing is all play to them."

I stare up at the reporter. Is that all this visitor is going to do? Sit around and talk with Mom? I thump my tail and pose prettily. But that reporter just keeps on talking. And *not* about me!

"Chewy has become quite the celebrity since his last movie!" the reporter says. "And haven't there been lots of German shepherds who have

starred in films—like Rin Tin Tin and Strongheart and Ace the Wonder Dog?"

"Yes, that's true. German shepherds like Chewy have been in films since the silent movie days, playing both friendly and fearsome characters," Mom says.

Chewy whines and nudges the reporter, coaxing her to pet him. *Humph!* Now that Chewy has warmed up to our guests, he's so impatient! But for some reason, the reporter doesn't seem to mind. In fact, she laughs!

"I have to say, I can't imagine this charmer playing a tough guy," she says.

"Oh, he has quite a range. Would you like Chewy to show you what he can do?" Mom asks.

Why is this all about Chewy? I think. I run over, pick up my blankie, and prance, but no one seems to notice.

"Chewy, speak," Mom says, and Chewy lets out some loud and fearsome barks.

GRROUFF, GROUFF!

Hey, I have a great bark too! I helpfully show off *my* bark.

Erruf! Erruf!

"And you may have seen Chewy do this trick in his latest movie, *Strike Out*," Mom continues. "The film is about a pro baseball player, and Chewy plays his dog, Sport. In that movie, whenever the player gets discouraged about his career, Sport cheers him up this way. Aidan, you got this?"

Aidan nods, grabs a baseball cap, and sets it on a chair. Then he gives a command: "Chewy, get the cap!"

The camera is rolling as Chewy gently picks up the cap in his mouth. He brings it to Aidan, nuzzling his hand until Aidan takes the cap and puts it on.

Ugh! Can't anyone else see Chewy's slobber on that hat?

"Wow," says the reporter. "That's impressive!"

That's nothing, I think. *Let me show you what I can do!*

I run to the teacup that's still on the floor.

Here I go, Aidan! It's our special trick!

I sit prettily next to the teacup, and with one dainty swipe of my paw, I tip it over. I wait for a response, but no one seems to notice. So I go big! I knock over the pitcher of water Aidan left on the floor, too, for good measure.

Uh-oh!

Now there's water everywhere. The floor is slick and slippery, and the kitchen rug is soaked. And Aidan isn't happy.

"Oh, Bella!" he cries as he rushes over to mop up the mess.

But those newspeople—they don't even glance my way. They're way too busy watching Chewy.

After a few moments, I figure it's no use. Obviously, it's all about Chewy today.

I slink away and settle myself in a corner with a big sigh.

Aidan finishes mopping up my mess and leaves for school, but that news crew still doesn't budge. They stay, talking and fussing over Chewy.

I grumble a little to myself as I close my eyes.

It's a while later when the news crew finally packs up.

"Thanks for agreeing to meet with us so early," the reporter says. "We have a quick deadline on this one. We hope to have it edited and on tonight's six o'clock news."

"Well, that was fun," Mom says to us after the door closes behind the visitors. "And I think you both impressed them. Now...are my two favorite star dogs ready to go do some film work today?"

My ears perk up.

Wait, what?

Are both Chewy and I working with Mom today? That's never happened before!

Suddenly, this day is looking *much* brighter.

Chapter 4

Doggy Dreams

Next thing I know, Mom is loading Chewy and me into our crates in her van so we can travel safely. I settle down for the ride.

I am relieved that I wasn't left home this time. I have so much fun going to do film work with Mom!

As I rest in the rumbling van, I wonder if today will be like the first time Mom and I worked on filming something together. On that outing, I had the chance to really show off my stuff!

For weeks before that day, we had daily practice sessions. Mom worked with me at the dog-training school and at home on a very different kind of trick. I learned how to bite on a T-shirt and hold it in my mouth as I hopped through things—a little hoop or a doggy door we have at home.

On the first afternoon that we were trying out the trick, Aidan came home and looked surprised. "Is that my old tee shirt? What's up?" he asked.

I remember hearing excitement in Mom's voice. "I got an email from the casting agency," she said. "When I first signed Bella up, I told the agency about all her talents and habits— like how she pulls her blankie all around the house. Now an advertising firm is looking for a small dog to drag a shirt outside for a laundry-detergent commercial."

"Bella, you were born for this role!" Aidan said, scratching me behind my ears. "Who knew that prancing around with a blankie would be just the skill needed for your first job!"

After we worked on that trick for a long time, Mom brought me early to a place I'd never been before.

I sniffed around to investigate. We were in a backyard, but not like any backyard I had seen before. I saw big, boxy metal things on little legs that I later learned were cameras. Strangest of all, someone held a furry-looking thing stuck on a stick. If I were taller, I would have jumped up and grabbed it—it looked like a giant fuzzy mouse toy!

Mom saw me staring and laughed.

"That's a microphone," she said. "That's how they'll record your bark at the end of the scene."

While I explored this new place, a crew member brought out a hose and a bag of dirt. He started making a big mud puddle in the yard.

For my big scene, I waited inside the house. But not Mom. Poor Mom ended up crouching outside right in the mud!

When I heard Mom's command, "Get the shirt," I did just that, grabbing it with my teeth. When she said, "Come, Bella," I popped through that doggy door—but the shirt I was carrying got snagged on the doorframe.

Still, I knew what was expected of me!

Get the shirt through the door, I told myself.

I pulled and pulled on that shirt...until I heard a ripping sound.

Oops.

The director called, "Cut."

Some people came and took the ripped shirt away and replaced it with another one.

How strange! I thought. When one of us dogs rips something up at home, no one ever runs to

34

give us another one.

We started the trick all over again. But the next time—I nailed it! With my teeth clamped on the shirt, I sailed through the doggy door like a champ!

I followed Mom's commands, dragged that shirt outside, and dumped it right in the mud puddle. Then I added a little something of my own, something I had *not* been taught. For good measure, I turned and flicked my back paw, sending even more mud clumping onto the dirty shirt.

The director yelled, "Cut," and the crew gave a cheer.

"That's my Bella," said Mom as she fed me a treat. "Always bringing that big personality. The director absolutely loves that extra bit you did with the mud."

It was many days later that Aidan called me excitedly to the living room.

"Bella, come see your commercial!" he said.

What's a commercial? I wondered as I trotted over.

There on the screen, I watched an adorable little white-and-copper dog jump through a doggy door with a shirt in her mouth.

Hey, that's me, I thought. *And my goodness, I do look amazing!*

So I guess that's what all that training and

practice with Mom and performing in front of people and funny-looking equipment leads to.

I was the star of a thing called a commercial. That's when I knew that being an actor dog suits me just fine!

I am dreamily recalling that day when the van stops and the engine cuts off. Mom slides open the door.

"We're here!" she says cheerfully. Inside my crate, I jump to my feet.

I'm wondering where "here" is. And I wonder what will happen today, with Chewy and me both showing up.

Mom opens our crates and snaps a leash to each of us dogs. I guess we are about to find out!

Chapter 5

Star Treatment

We're only at the studio a few moments when a man, Mr. Shah, introduces himself to Mom. He greets us dogs too. He's from an organization called American Humane. I've met people from American Humane before on the sets of my commercials. I know why he's here—to make sure that Chewy and I and any other animals are safe and well cared for during filming. He won't let a studio make us work too hard or too long, or do anything dangerous. Of course, Mom wouldn't allow that either.

Next, we meet the person everyone is calling "director." She wears glasses that she keeps putting on and taking off, and has almost as much energy as me.

"I love this script," I hear the director tell Mom. "It's based on my favorite book when I was growing up, *Life with Lollipop*. It's about a family with a very special dog named, well, Lollipop, of course. It's been my dream to make this into a series. I am so excited that Bella here will help bring the story to life."

Hey, director, I don't know what a series is, but I'm excited too! I think.

"It was a challenge to cast the dogs for this show, because Lollipop has so many scenes," the director says to Mom. "We don't want to overwork one dog, and we need to show both Lollipop's tenderness and courageousness. So we cast three dogs."

Now I'm really confused. Chewy and I aren't playing the same dog, are we?

"There's a puppy to play Lollipop as a young dog," the director continues. "We've already filmed those scenes, so she's not on set today. Then there's Crusher, a Jack Russell terrier who works with another trainer. He is very athletic and will do the more physical, energetic scenes. And then there's your Bella here."

I hear my name and look up.

"Just look at that face!" the director says. "She will be in the scenes that melt viewers' hearts."

At first, I'm very happy to hear *I'll* be playing Lollipop.

But wait a minute! I think. *In my commercial, I was the star, the top dog! Now three of us are sharing the billing? Why can't I do the energetic, athletic scenes?*

Then something else happens that I'm not expecting.

"We'll have to send Bella to makeup," the director says. "Crusher has a white patch on the top of his head. We'll just add a bit of doggy-safe makeup so Bella and Crusher look the same."

Makeup? That stuff humans put on to make themselves look different? My goodness, I don't need any stinky makeup! I'm perfect the way I am!

Mom takes Chewy to wait in a comfy kennel and then brings me to another room and lifts me into a makeup chair. A woman starts sweeping a soft brush across the top of my head.

Hey, that tickles!

I'm annoyed at first.

But then I look around. In the next chair, a human girl is seated. She's just about Aidan's age. I see she's having her hair and makeup done, too, and she doesn't look upset at all. She looks excited!

"Hi, little dog," the girl says. "You are sooo

cute! I'm Justine. I'm in *Life with Lollipop* too.
I'm just going over the script for our big scene
later today!" she says, holding up a black binder.

Mom introduces me. "This is Bella. And this
is her first ever series."

"Mine too!" says Justine. "I can't wait to work with you, Bella."

Her voice sounds so nice that I wag my tail when I hear my name.

Maybe this isn't so bad, I decide. After all, I'm warm and comfy, Mom is close by, and nice people are fussing over me.

I guess this is just part of the star treatment I deserve!

And that tickly makeup brush—I guess that's okay too. In fact, it's kind of scratching an itch!

Chapter 6
Mirror Image

Once they put the finishing touches on my fur and makeup, I'm ready to go.

"One more thing, Bella," Mom says. "Your costume!"

Mom lifts me from the chair and brings me to another room. She begins fitting a fluffy tutu on me! I've worn this before at home. At the time, I thought it was just for fun. I guess Mom was getting me used to my costume, to make sure

it was comfy and wouldn't distract me when it was time to work.

Now, with makeup and a frilly costume, I truly feel like a star! Mom attaches my leash and I flounce out of the room—and that's when I spot him! I see a dog that looks like me, standing all by himself in a corner.

No leash? No handler nearby? That's unusual for a film set, I think.

But there's something else that makes me curious. This dog is standing perfectly still. Could this be Crusher? The dog everyone says is so lively and athletic?

And also, why can't I smell another dog in this room?

Mom sees me looking that way. "Want to go meet him?" she asks.

She holds my leash but lets me take the lead.

I get close to the dog, circle around, and stare him straight in the eye.

It's a bit like looking in the mirror. This dog has white-and-copper coloring around his face like I do. He also has a white patch on his head, like the one the makeup people added to my fur.

But one sniff tells me this isn't a real dog at all.

I put out my paw to touch it. It doesn't growl or nip at me. And it feels a bit like my fuzzy mouse toy!

Mom laughs when she sees my confusion.

"Bella, meet Stuffy. It's a type of stuffed animal, made by the props department to look like you and Crusher. Stuffy will stand in for you for any dangerous scenes. Think of him as your stunt double. I heard Stuffy has a scene with a

real snake in this series!"

Well, my goodness, I think. *A life-size doggy doll of me!*

I give Stuffy a few more sniffs.

"Also, you'll be grateful when they bring Stuffy on the set to check the scene and set up the lighting," says Mom. "Then you won't have to sit still while the lighting crew does all their adjustments."

Good! If this pretend dog is going to take on all the dangerous work and the boring stuff, then Stuffy is okay with me.

"Now if you two are quite through getting acquainted, we need to keep to our schedule."

Mom heads with me to Chewy's kennel. "Time for your scene together," she says as she leads us both to a film set.

Hey, wait a minute, I think. *It's one thing to*

share the spotlight with two dogs and a stuffed animal. They don't expect me to work with Chewy, do they?

This is *not* what I had in mind.

Chapter 7

Best Buddies?

Mom brings us to a set that looks like our living room at home—if someone smashed down and hauled away one of the walls! There's a couch, some chairs, a rug, and a fireplace. But where the ceiling should be, there are bright lights shining down. In place of the missing wall, there are more lights, plus cameras on wheels, and those funny microphones on sticks. Lots of people move about.

Some dogs might be a little skittish in a place like this, but Chewy and I are pros. We're used to it!

Also, not far away is a big table practically overflowing with food for the actors and crew to munch on. One sniff tells me that there's cheese and meat and bread and fruit and other

goodies. It smells heavenly! But as a showbiz dog, I've had to learn not to be distracted by the tempting food scents in the air.

Chewy, though, still needs to work on this skill. His nose is in the air, and he's tugging at his leash. Typical.

"Not now, Chewy. You're on the job," Mom reminds him.

As Chewy and I check out the set and get comfortable, the director comes out to talk to the crew.

"This scene is very short, but it shows how spunky our Lollipop is. And we were fortunate to find a Jack Russell terrier and a German shepherd who are good friends and can work together. May I introduce...Bella and Chewy."

"Hey, Bella. Hey, Chewy," someone calls out.

"Our trainer, Sarah Jameson, tells me these two doggy siblings were raised together, so they're best buddies," the director says.

Best buddies? I don't know about that! I think.

"In this scene, our Lollipop, played by Bella here, is going to show just how spunky she is," the director continues. "When a big dog visits her home and takes her favorite toy, Lollipop grabs it right back, sets it down, and barks right in the big dog's face! That big dog, of course, is Chewy."

Some of the crew members nod and smile.

When everyone is ready, we start the scene. First, Mom brings Chewy the toy and gives a command for him to stay. She gives a click to let him know he got it right.

Then Mom says, "Bella, get the toy." I know

that means it's time for me to hop up (I'm great at jumping!) and take the toy right from Chewy's mouth.

Finally, Mom says, "Speak, Bella," and I drop the toy and bark at Chewy.

It's funny, but Chewy and I do this same thing in real life—like this morning, when he stole my fuzzy mouse toy. The director probably doesn't

know that Mom started with something we already do, and taught us to do it on command.

The director asks for several takes. That means she wants us to do it over and over. I know that it's not because we're getting it wrong. She just wants lots of choices so she can pick which one works best for the story she's trying to tell.

It turns out working with Chewy isn't so bad. I have to admit, he does look noble and regal and maybe a little fearsome, staring down at me. And as much as he loves food, he doesn't let that table full of yummies down the hall mess with his focus once we begin the scene. Maybe he does have a bit of star quality like Rin Tin Tin and Strongheart.

And, if I'm being honest, Chewy makes me look good—like I'm a feisty pup afraid of no one. I don't know if I'd be quite so brave, grabbing a toy from another big dog. I guess I'm grateful to Chewy for that!

Once the shot is done, Chewy bounds toward me, all proud and playful.

Yes, Chewy. We were great! I think. But I know it's not time to romp yet. Mom leads Chewy and me to our bowls, and we lap up some water. As I lick my lips, Mom carefully changes me out of my tutu costume. She fits a dog-friendly pointed hat on my head.

"Now, Chewy, you get to go back to the kennel and relax. And, Bella, you're all ready for your birthday tea-party scene," Mom says.

Once Chewy is settled, Mom walks me to an outside set. It's pretty and green with trees and flowers and benches, just like a public park. I see the prop people setting up teacups on a picnic blanket spread out on the ground.

I know what that means! It's finally time to perform the special tip-it trick that Aidan taught me. The one I promised to get just right!

I'm not worried. After all, Aidan and I practiced over and over.

What could possibly go wrong?

Chapter 8

Tipping Point

Mom brings me over to the checkered picnic blanket. It's a pretty sight! There are a few plates, a picnic basket, and some plastic teacups filled with a dark liquid. And there's a fancy birthday cake, set right in the middle.

Soon the young actor, Justine, joins us. She greets me, but then she looks over at Mom. I can tell she wants to ask her a question.

"I've seen you talking to your dogs today,"

Justine finally begins. "And I just wonder—do you think they understand what people say?"

Mom smiles at her. "I guess I do tend to talk a lot to Bella and Chewy and the dogs I train at the school. It's a habit of mine. But I believe dogs may understand more than most people realize."

Mom leans over to scratch behind my ear. "Of course, many dogs learn to recognize some words and phrases and commands. But it's

not just our words that communicate—it's the tone of our voice and the expression on our face that they read too. And you know, I have found that sometimes it seems like dogs have a special talent. They can almost sense what we're feeling."

Justine nods as if she's thinking this over.

"Well then," says Justine, "if it's okay with you, I'm going to explain something to Bella—even if she doesn't quite get what I'm saying. Even if it only makes *me* feel better."

"Sure," says Mom. "Go ahead."

Justine crouches next to me.

"Bella, we're about to film a scene together. And just so you know, when I yell, 'Oh no, how could you?' I'm going to sound angry. But I'm only pretending to be mad. It's just a line I have to say."

Justine gives me a gentle pat on my back. "The script says that you…" She stops and laughs. "I mean *Lollipop* ruins my character's birthday picnic by knocking over a teacup and spilling grape juice on her new dress. But I want you to know—no matter how loud or upset I sound today, I still like you."

Justine's voice is so kind, I give her my paw.

I like you too, I think.

Soon another actor joins us on the picnic blanket. "Bella, this is Carol," Justine says. "She is playing my grandma in the birthday party scene."

"Hello, little pup," Carol says to me.

Just before the camera rolls, Mom tucks herself out of sight behind a tree.

I see the teacup and know this is it—my big moment. The one Aidan said will make me a star! And my chance to make Mom and Aidan proud.

Mom says the command, "Tip it."

I'm ready! I lift my paw, but for some reason, I miss the teacup! Maybe it's because things are just a little different—I am on a blanket spread over grass, instead of the tile floor I practiced on at home. Could that have messed with my aim?

"No problem, Bella," Mom calls out. "We'll try again."

We begin again, and I hear the tip-it command. I move my paw toward the cup. Somehow, though, my foot lands *inside* the cup! I am so surprised to feel something cool and wet on my paw that I jump back—right onto the birthday cake!

I turn around. Now there are grape-juice paw prints on the picnic blanket and pink frosting all over me.

"Cut," the director says. Her shoulders slump, and she pulls off her glasses. Even though the director smiles at me, I can tell she's disappointed.

There's a fuss as a prop person whisks away the cake to try to repair the damage, and someone else comes running over with a new

picnic blanket. The whole scene has to be reset again.

I hang my head. Aidan is counting on me to get this trick right. He wants to prove that he's got what it takes to be a dog trainer. And I've failed him. Twice.

Mom comes over to comfort me. She gently wipes off my paws and fur with a soft cloth. "Bella, you know things don't always go well on the first try," she says. "You'll get this! I believe in you."

"Me too, Bella," Justine says as she settles herself back onto the new blanket. The actor playing Grandma returns too. Mom once again tucks herself behind the tree.

I'm determined to get it right this time— for Justine, for Mom, for the nice director, but especially for Aidan.

I hear the director call out, "Rolling." A sound person says, "Sound speed." Then the director says, "Action."

The two actors speak some words to each other. I hear Mom call out the tip-it command to me.

I swing my paw forward—and the cup tips over. The juice splashes out right onto Justine's dress. I hear a click coming from Mom, and I know everything went just as it was supposed to!

Justine gasps. "Lollipop! Oh no, how could you?" she cries.

Somehow I know just what to do, just what will make this scene extra special. I put my paw on Justine's hand and raise my head. I look into her eyes to show everyone how sorry Lollipop is that someone she loves is upset.

Are you getting this, cameraperson? I think. *This is some good stuff!*

Then Mom quietly gives the command "Come here, Bella," and I run from Justine as if my character, Lollipop, is sad and embarrassed.

At the end of the scene, Mom hurries over with my liver treats.

"Did you train her to do that? To reach out with an apologetic paw like that?" the director asks Mom. "It's like she's actually saying she's sorry."

Mom laughs. "No. I guess I should have warned you that our Bella improvises."

"Well, I'm glad," the director says. "That's even better than what was in the script. What a truly amazing dog."

Chapter 9

To the Rescue!

"That's a wrap for us today, Bella," Mom tells me.

We are heading to makeup to get the spot shampooed off my head when a crew person finds us. He's out of breath.

"The director asks if you'll come back to the set," the man says. "Crusher is having a tough time with his scene. She wondered if Bella would give it a shot. We need to finish this afternoon to stay on schedule."

"But Bella hasn't trained for that scene," Mom says.

The crew person nods. "Right, but the director has seen Bella's laundry detergent commercial. You know, where she drags the shirt into the mud? This is kind of like that. Do you think she'd remember those commands well enough to follow them for this scene?"

"We can try," Mom says. And back we go to the set. Justine and the grandmother actor are gone now. But the director and crew still shuffle about. And I catch a glimpse of Crusher and his handler as they are leaving. Well, what do you know? Crusher does look almost as adorable as me!

When she sees us, the director rushes up. "Let

me bring you up to speed," she says to Mom. "This scene takes place after Lollipop runs away from the tea party. She's lost her birthday hat, but she comes back to the park looking for her family. Instead, she finds a young mom who has laid her sleeping baby on a little blanket."

The director points to a piece of cloth on the ground. I notice something long and squiggly in the grass near it. I creep as close as my leash

will allow. *Whoa!* The thing in the grass looks like a creature—maybe a dangerous creature! But it smells strange...and kind of rubbery.

"Our spunky Lollipop looks over at the baby and senses danger and—*bam!*" the director says so suddenly that I jump.

"Lollipop spots a poisonous snake near the baby's blanket and dashes in to save the day." The director turns to me. "Don't worry, Bella. We're using a very lifelike doll for the baby. And that snake is just a prop. We'll bring in Stuffy to film with the real snake later. But I promise you, you'll be the hero of this scene."

"Wow! Sounds exciting," says Mom.

"We've got great footage of Crusher rushing back to save the baby. He leaped over that fallen log over there like a gazelle! But Crusher doesn't want to have anything to do with the blanket or the baby doll. We can't get him to do the action the script calls for."

The director shakes her head. "Someone walked near the set with a hot pastrami sandwich, and I think maybe the good smells got to him. He couldn't seem to concentrate. Do you think you and Bella could give it a try?" she asks.

"What do you need Bella to do, exactly?" Mom asks.

While Mom and the director talk, I give the squiggly thing in the grass one last sniff.

You might not be real, but I'm keeping my eye on you!

Soon Mom calls me back and unclips the leash.

A camera rolls in a bit closer toward me.

The director calls, "Action."

Mom gives the command. "Get the shirt, Bella."

Huh?

I look around, confused. There's no shirt. But there's a piece of cloth on the ground that looks a bit like a shirt. And a bit like my blankie. It's not far from that creepy fake snake. I grab the cloth with my teeth, but I can't lift it up because the baby doll is weighing it down.

So I do what I can. With my head low to the ground and my tail end in the air, I tug and tug

with all my might! I pull that cloth until it finally moves bit by bit away from that thing in the grass.

When the director calls, "Cut," I stop and look up. Have I done well? Or will Mom be disappointed that I wasn't strong enough to pick up the cloth, like I did for the commercial?

I guess I did okay! Mom comes over, full of praise and bringing treats.

Then the director rushes toward us. "Thank you both," she says. "You saved the day. Now we have Lollipop rescuing the baby on film! Our viewers will love that!" She crouches down and rubs my head. "They'll love you, Bella!"

Chapter 10
Two Stars, One Home

When we finally head home, I'm tired but happy.

Mom bursts through the door with both Chewy and me at her side. She's just as excited as I am.

"Aidan, Bella did it! The tip-it trick you taught her was a hit! There were a few little problems at first…"

"Oh no!" Aidan says.

"No, it's okay!" Mom says. "It only took a couple takes, and then Bella was perfect. That teacup went right over like it was supposed to. You know things don't always work on the first try, even for the human actors. But Bella got it— that's what's important. Aidan, you're becoming a great dog trainer."

The smile that lights up Aidan's face means the world to me.

"What's more, Bella stepped up when another dog had trouble with a command," Mom says. "So now not only will Bella be in the heartfelt scenes, but she's in a heroic scene too. The director is thinking about expanding her role. That's how good she was!"

I bask in all this praise.

But you know, I kind of feel bad for Chewy.

No one is talking about him. Even if his role today was small, he was impressive! I press my nose to Mom's leg, then go and sit by Chewy.

When Mom glances toward the two of us, it's as if she remembers Chewy's great performance too. She smiles our way.

"Both our dogs shone like the stars they are today," Mom says. "They are quite the talented twosome."

Her proud voice makes my tail wag.

Mom lets us out in the yard then, and Chewy and I have the best playtime. We sniff, chase, and explore. By the time we come back inside, we're both panting. It's been such a great day, I don't even mind when I see Chewy sneak my mouse toy over to his doggy bed.

A little later, Aidan calls everyone to the living room. We all squash onto the couch together as the news comes on the TV.

Aidan points at the television.

"Chewy, Bella, look! Here's the story about you and Mom!"

I see the reporter from this morning smiling

on the screen. There are lots of film clips of Chewy, but surprisingly, some of me, too, looking up at the camera.

My goodness, I do look adorable!

The reporter does a lot of the talking. I guess that's what reporters do! But then I hear Mom's

voice from the television speaker, and Mom's image flashes on the screen.

"I'm so grateful these dogs are part of my family," Mom says. "And they play such an important role in bringing to life some amazing stories on film. After all, it's stories that help us

learn about the world."

Wow! I think. *Is that what we do?*

Mom's voice continues from the speaker. "And maybe watching our dogs on TV or at the movie theater will remind people that there are furry companions, like these two, waiting in shelters to be adopted into loving homes."

The reporter shows up on the screen again, smiling. "Well, there you have it," she says. "Two doggy stars from the same home here in Atlanta—one small and plucky, the other large and lovable. At first glance they may seem as different as can be, but they're both living their best lives as companions and on-screen sensations. And they're having a doggone good time doing it."

I guess Chewy and I are pretty good friends even if we are so different, I think as I snuggle on the coach with Mom and Dad and Aidan and Chewy too. Plus, like Mom said, we're family. And I'm just about as happy and proud about that as I can be.

In France in 1895, during one of the first films ever made, a giant mastiff bound into a scene of workers leaving a factory. The dog was not an actor, but he did unknowingly put himself into film history. Ever since, human's best friend has been finding ways to steal the show.

As filmmaking grew, so did the ways in which dogs were brought into them. People began to train dogs as actors. One of the first doggy stars appeared in 1922. The German shepherd Rin Tin Tin, or "Rinty," had been rescued by an American soldier during World War I. But it wasn't until after the war that the dog became an international celebrity. Starring in twenty-three films, Rin Tin Tin was not only the most famous dog actor of the silent film era, he was one of the most famous actors of any kind!

Eventually, films featured sound and color, and showbiz dogs got even more opportunities to show their stuff. In 1939, a Cairn terrier named Terry got her big break. As Toto, she accompanied Dorothy to the Land of Oz in *The Wizard of Oz*, and became the first doggy star in a movie filmed in color.

Dogs' roles in film continued to grow through the mid-twentieth century. Companies began to specialize in training animal actors. For Chris, a 200-pound Saint Bernard, drooling and shedding was nothing new, but for his role in the 1992 movie *Beethoven*, he also needed to be quick and energetic and perform tricks. Chris was so successful at learning his new skills, a sequel was made with him as the star!

But as dogs were asked to do more and more on set, rules needed to be put in place to help keep them safe. Animal rights groups created guidelines for film companies to follow when working with animal actors. This helped ensure that dogs remained safe on set and could live long and happy lives once they were done acting.

Today, actor dogs' roles continue to change. Computer graphics can be used to keep real dogs out of scenes that might be unsafe. But while technology can now imitate dogs on screen, nothing can replace the personality, unpredictability, and joy they bring to the set.

Unlike many working dogs, actor dogs come in all shapes, sizes, and breeds. But for every showbiz dog, much skill and training is required for each film-worthy performance.

No matter if the part calls for a dog to sit still or do a complex trick, all actor dogs need to be able to follow instructions and have strong self-control. They also need to be comfortable around their fellow human actors and any other animals that may be on set.

Dogs are selected for roles based on their appearance, personality, and skill. Often, more than one dog is cast for a single part. This may be done to highlight different traits or to show a dog growing older over time. Some dogs are brought on as stunt doubles. Other times, a dog might have an understudy—a dog that can step in, in case of emergency.

Dogs of all ages can work as actor dogs, and some act well into old age. Often, actor dogs retire to the homes of their trainers, or with other humans they have worked with whose hearts they have captured.

Actor Dogs in This Book

Jack Russell Terrier

These big-hearted dogs began as fox hunters bred by John "Jack" Russell. Today, their bold nature makes them great actors and delightful companions.

Height: 10–12 inches
Weight: 9–15 pounds
Life Span: 12–14 years
Coat: White with black or tan markings
Known for: Alertness, curiosity

German Shepherd

The German shepherd was first bred to herd sheep in Germany. But the dog's smarts, speed, and strength have made it a popular choice for many other jobs— from police work to acting—around the world.

Height: 22–26 inches
Weight: 50–90 pounds
Life Span: 7–10 years
Coat: Black and cream or tan
Known for: Confidence, courage

Breed information based on American Kennel Club data. For more on these and other breeds, visit www.akc.org/dog-breeds/.

Acknowledgments

I am so very grateful to Greg Tresan, owner, animal coordinator, and trainer with Animal Casting Atlanta, for generously sharing information with me about showbiz dogs and for answering my many questions. Mr. Tresan also kindly met with me at his training and boarding facility, Atlanta Dogworks, one November day and introduced me to Penny, a joyful, talented Jack Russell terrier with an impressive film and commercial résumé. Together, Mr. Tresan and Penny demonstrated the kind of teamwork, training, and "play" that results in some amazing canine performances on the big and little screen!

Catherine Stier recalls being charmed by the dogs she saw in movies as a child. As a grown-up researching this book, Stier met a real live doggy movie star and learned about the kind of "play" and training that prepares a pup to become an on-screen celebrity. This is Stier's fourth book in the A Dog's Day series. She is also the author of several award-winning picture books for children.

Francesca Rosa was born in Italy and is a graduate of the School of Comics and Illustration in Milan. Since childhood, she has had an infinite love for animals, and they frequently appear in her illustrated books. Francesca's work has been published in Italy, Korea, China, England, and the United States. She currently lives in Italy with her husband, and her dog, Milù.